Little
Stupendo
Flies High

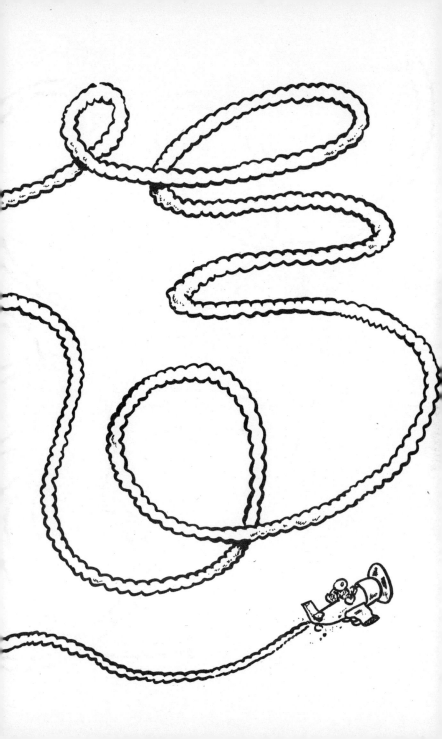

Books by the same author

Little Stupendo
Little Stupendo Rides Again
Oshie

Little Stupendo
Flies High

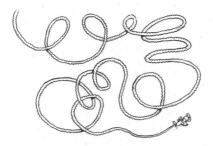

Jon Blake
Illustratedby Martin Chatterton

WALKER
BOOKS

First published 2001 by Walker Books Ltd
87 Vauxhall Walk, London SE11 5HJ

Sprinters edition published in hardback by Heinemann Library,
a division of Reed Educational and Professional Publishing Limited,
by arrangement with Walker Books Ltd

This edition published 2017

2 4 6 8 10 9 7 5 3 1

This book has been typeset in Garamond

Printed in Great Britain by Clays Ltd, St Ives plc

British Library Cataloguing in Publication Data:
a catalogue record for this book is available from the British Library

ISBN 978-1-4063-7871-9

www.walker.co.uk

CONTENTS

CHAPTER ONE

Everyone needs a holiday. Even the world's greatest stunt artist. That's why Little Stupendo was sunning herself on the beach at Malibu, outside her Aunt Juno's beach hut.

"This is the life," said Little Stupendo. "I wonder what Dad's doing?"

This is what the Great Stupendo was doing – banging his head on the wall. Then he wrung his hands. Then he stamped his feet.

"Why isn't she back yet?" he cried. "I've got a stunt tomorrow, and I need help!"

The Great Stupendo rang his old friend, Marvo the Memory Man, to see if he could help.

Marvo was famous for his fantastic memory act. The trouble was, Marvo was getting older. His memory wasn't what it used to be. In fact, it was next to useless.

"Hello," said Marvo, "this is Albert Hall. No, not Albert Hall. Frank Tomato. No, that's not right either."

"Marvo?" said the Great Stupendo. "This is your old friend, the Great Stupendo."

"Ah, Great Stupendo!" said Marvo. "Who?"

The Great Stupendo wondered if this was such a good idea.

Next day, Marvo and the Great Stupendo dragged a mattress to the Market Square, where a crowd was gathering.

"Right," said the Great Stupendo. "You keep the crowd back, while I climb to the top of City Hall."

"Climb to the top of City Hall?" said Marvo. "Why?"

"So I can jump off it!" said the Great Stupendo, who was getting very impatient with Marvo.

"Jump off it," said Marvo. "Right, I see."

With that, the Great Stupendo put on his sticky-fly boots and climbed right up the side of City Hall. The crowd went quiet. The Great Stupendo prepared to jump.

Meanwhile, Marvo was looking at the mattress with a frown on his face.

"Who's dumped this in the square?" he grizzled.

Marvo took hold of the mattress and began to drag it away.

Just then, Marvo heard a loud noise behind him.

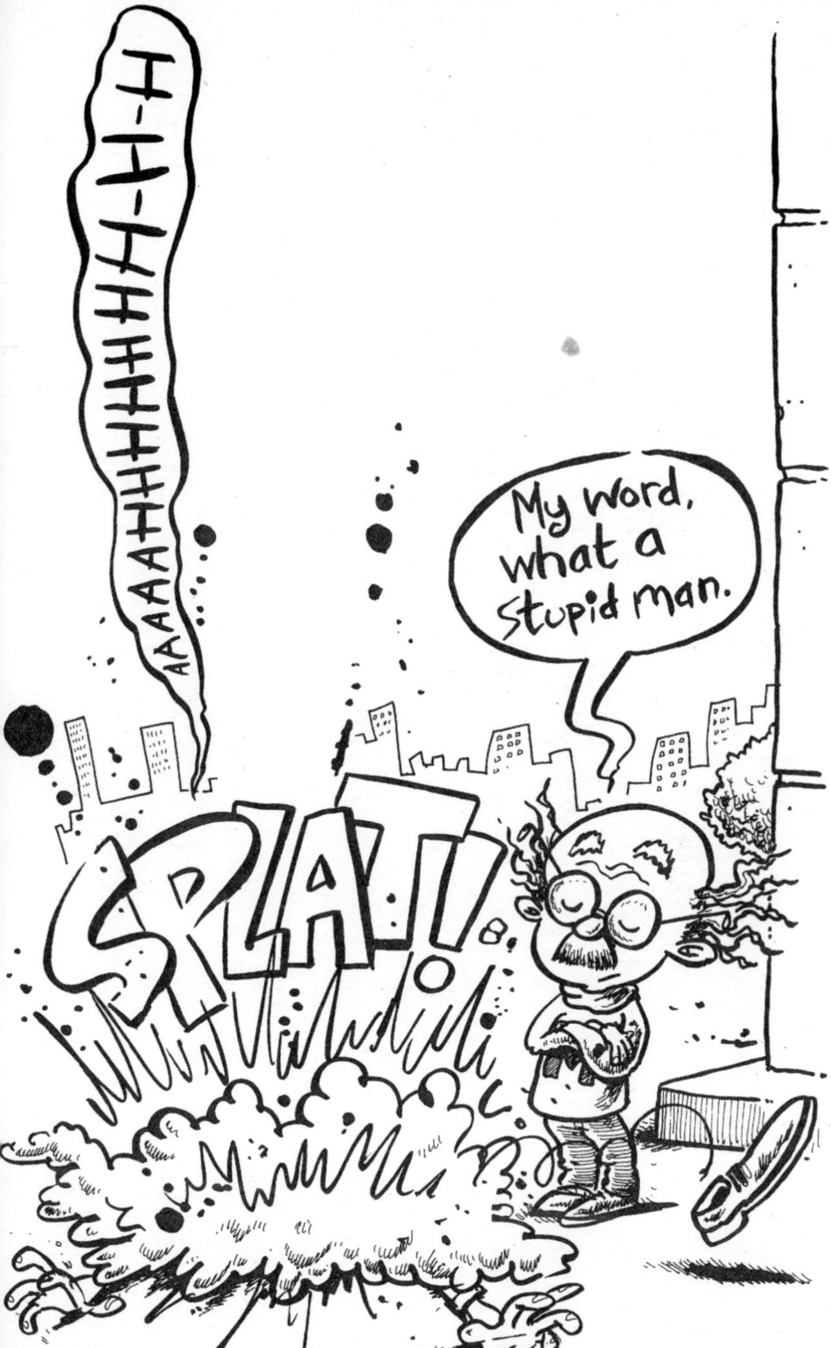

AAAAAAAAHHHHHHHHHHHH-H-H-H-H
My word, what a stupid man.
SPLAT!

CHAPTER TWO

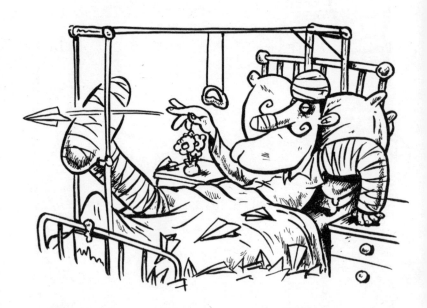

The Great Stupendo looked a sorry sight at the City Hospital. He couldn't do anything except make paper planes. He'd made about three hundred so far. The room was knee-deep in them.

"I'm so bored!" he moaned.

Just then the door opened, and in walked Little Stupendo. She was relaxed and tanned after her holiday with Aunt Juno.

"How are we going to do our act now?" said Little Stupendo.

"We aren't," croaked the Great Stupendo. "Not for ten weeks."

"Ten weeks!?" cried Little Stupendo. It seemed like a lifetime.

"You could always knit," replied the Great Stupendo.

Little Stupendo pulled a sick face. "How many times must I tell you?" she said. "I hate knitting! I want *action*!"

"But you can't do stunts on your own," said the Great Stupendo.

"Why not?" said Little Stupendo.

"Because," said the Great Stupendo.

"Because what?" asked Little Stupendo.

The Great Stupendo smiled, placed his big hand on her little hand, and put on a look of great wisdom. "Just because," he said.

Little Stupendo fumed. She *hated* it when he said that. It made her even more determined to prove she could do stunts on her own.

Little Stupendo began to imagine the new acts she could work on…

Little Stupendo began to feel miserable. None of her ideas were going to work. But just then, she reached into her pocket, and pulled out one of her dad's paper planes.

That's it! she thought to herself. *I'll do aeroplane stunts!*

Little Stupendo looked up
FLYING SCHOOLS in Phony Pages.
There was only one advert:

Little Stupendo didn't much like the sound of this flying school. But, as it was the only one, she decided to give it a go.

CHAPTER THREE

Soon, Little Stupendo found herself in a big, lumpy field, with nothing in it but a barn and a caravan.

Suddenly the caravan door burst open and there stood a sneaky-faced man in an old flying jacket. "Welcome!" he cried. "Give me all your money and I'll show you to the plane."

Little Stupendo did as she was asked, and Sid Honest led her to the big barn.

There inside was the oldest plane she had ever seen.

Little Stupendo climbed into the pilot's seat. Sid Honest handed her a flying helmet and a book called *How to Fly in One Quick Lesson*.

The noise of the engine drowned out Little Stupendo's words. The old plane started bumping crazily over the field, with the engine spluttering.

Little Stupendo flicked through the pages of *How to Fly in One Quick Lesson*. She twisted this, she tweaked that, and she pulled on the joystick with all her might. The plane gave a little hop, then a jump, then bumped back down. It just wouldn't take off.

Meanwhile, in the field next door, the vicar of St Peter's was having a very nice tea party. Everybody sat about in their very best clothes, using the very best china.

Suddenly…

"That's it," said Little Stupendo. "I'm going to find a proper aeroplane."

Later that day, she arrived at Hugeville International Airport.

"Now these are *real* planes," she said to herself, watching the mighty monsters take to the skies.

Up ahead was a huge building with a sign saying WORLDWIDE SUPERJET INC.

Little Stupendo
walked straight in
and asked to see the
manager.

"Can *I* be of assistance?"
barked a loud, chilling voice.

A tall woman stood
before Little Stupendo.
Her suit had huge
shoulders and her
hair was like
a crash-helmet.
"I am Angela Power,"
she boomed.
"Managing Director
of Worldwide
Superjet Inc."

35

"Can I fly one of your planes?"
asked Little Stupendo.

Angela Power laughed and
laughed, then patted Little Stupendo
on the head and laughed some
more.

Little Stupendo felt like giving up. But as she walked home, she remembered the conversation with her dad at the hospital:

Little Stupendo got angry all over again. She would show her dad, *and* that Angela Power!

Just then, Little Stupendo passed by Goosey Park. It was covered by a huge fair, full of lights and people and crazy rides. And there, right in the middle, was a machine called Virtual Flight.

Little Stupendo bought a ticket and got into the machine. To her delight, it was exactly like the cockpit of a big airliner.

In no time Little Stupendo was
at the controls, dipping the make-
believe wings, dropping the make-
believe wheels and landing on the
make-believe runway.

"This is brilliant!" cried
Little Stupendo. And she
ran all the way home
with her arms stretched
out like mighty wings.

But Little Stupendo wasn't finished yet. Oh no. Back home, she went straight for her piggy bank and filled her pockets with coins. Then she ran all the way back to the fair and paid for ninety-three goes on Virtual Flight

The crowd had all gone home. The lights of the fair were all out. But Little Stupendo was still at the controls of her make-believe plane.

CHAPTER FOUR

Next day, Little Stupendo marched
straight into Angela Power's office.

"I am Little Stupendo," she said.
"I know how to fly and I want to fly
your plane."

This time Angela Power did not laugh. "You again!" she said. She reached for the button marked Security Guards. Then she thought again.

"Maybe I *could* use you," she said.

Angela Power opened a cupboard and handed Little Stupendo a uniform. "Put this on," she said, "and report to the 10:30 flight to Addis Ababa."

Little Stupendo couldn't believe it. A pilot's uniform! She hurried to the toilets to try it on.

Little Stupendo was in for a nasty surprise. It wasn't a pilot's uniform at all. It was a flight attendant's uniform! Little Stupendo wouldn't be flying the plane – she'd be serving the tea!

At least I'll be on the plane, she thought.

The 10:30 to Addis Ababa took to the sky. It was a massive great plane, with hundreds of hungry passengers. Little Stupendo did her best to serve them, but she soon got fed up. You couldn't do many stunts when you were serving hot coffee, or balancing trays of Mississippi Mud Pie.

If only I could get in the pilot's cabin, she thought to herself.

But Little Stupendo couldn't even get *near* the pilot's cabin. She was run off her feet, all the way to Addis Ababa, *and* halfway back.

Then, out of the blue, Little Stupendo got her chance. All the passengers were asleep and the other flight attendants were putting their feet up. Little Stupendo crept to the front of the plane and poked her nose through the curtains. It looked fantastic. The two pilots sat at a great deck of controls, steering the plane through the clouds like a hot knife through butter.

Suddenly Captain Snow looked round. "Ah," he said. "Have you brought our hot milk?"

"A big dollop of syrup in mine, please," added Captain Sputnik.

Little Stupendo hurried back, fetched the captains' drinks and put them on the floor between them.

"Excuse me," she said, "but would you like another pilot?"

Captain Snow laughed. "Two is quite enough," he said.

"That's right," added Captain Sputnik. "If anything happens to Captain Snow, I can fly the plane, and if anything happens to me, Captain Snow can fly it."

"So nothing can go wrong," said Captain Snow.

With that, Captain Snow and Captain Sputnik both dived for their hot milk.

There was no time to lose. Little Stupendo seized the controls of the plane. At last!

She picked up the intercom:

"Ladies and gentlemen," she said. "This is your new captain speaking. I hope you are enjoying your flight. Please fasten your seatbelts as I will now be trying a few stunts."

With that, Little Stupendo took the
plane straight up like a rocket …

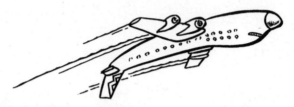

flew upside down …

dipped the wings …

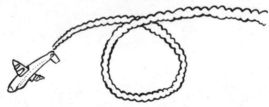

and looped the loop.

WARNING TO CHILDREN:
ALWAYS ASK PERMISSION FROM AN ADULT
BEFORE FLYING AN AIRLINER.

"This is madness!" cried Hester Prune from Tunbridge Wells.

"This is fun!" squealed her seven children.

Little Stupendo was having the time of her life. But there was a nasty surprise in store for her. A red warning light began to flash on the control panel.

"The fuel tank!" she gasped.

The plane was still miles from the airport. There was only one thing for it. Little Stupendo had to make an emergency landing.

Little Stupendo turned the plane and began to bring it down. It was then she saw the sign:

CITY HOSPITAL

That was where she was!

Meanwhile, the Great Stupendo was folding his nine-thousandth paper plane. As he looked out of the window, his eyes nearly popped out of his head.

Little Stupendo waggled her wings, and lowered her wheels, and aimed the aeroplane like a dart. All her hours of practice were paying off. Smooth as silk, she touched down and taxied down the make-do runway.

All over the hospital, doctors were dropping their pens, and patients were rushing to the windows.

"Wh-who's that at the controls?" asked the Great Stupendo.

The Great Stupendo gawked as the huge airliner came closer …

closer …

closer …

"Little Stupendo!" gasped the
Great Stupendo.

The great plane eased to a halt.
Little Stupendo waved to the crowd
that had gathered below. Then she
slid down the escape chute and did
a double-tuck somersault onto the
ground. There was a huge cheer.

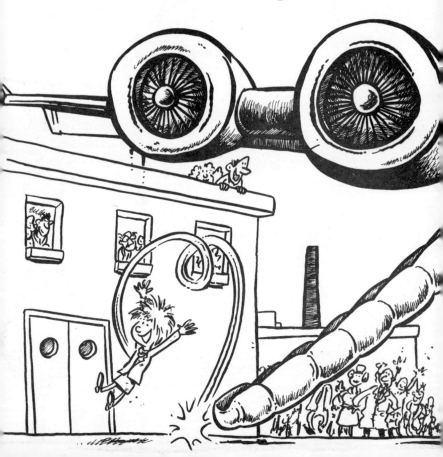

The Great Stupendo wheeled his way through the crowd, still in his pyjamas.

"Little Stupendo!" he said. "You … you flew *that*!"

Little Stupendo nodded happily and patted the aeroplane's giant wheel.

"Better than knitting, eh, Dad?"

Jon Blake started writing for children during his brief career as a teacher. Since then he has had a number of jobs, from community centre warden to part-time lecturer. He is the author of several books for young people, including *Oshie, The King of Rock and Roll* and *The Hell Hound of Hooley Street*, as well as the picture books *Impo* and *You're a Hero, Daley B!* He has written two other books about the famous Stupendos: *Little Stupendo*, which was shortlisted for the Children's Book Award, and *Little Stupendo Rides Again*. He has also written plays for television and the stage.